Go Green
by Recycling

Lisa Bullard   Illustrated by Wes Thomas

LERNER PUBLICATIONS ◆ MINNEAPOLIS

NOTE TO EDUCATORS

Find text recall questions at the end of each chapter. Critical-thinking and text feature questions are available on page 23. These help young readers learn to think critically about the topic by using the text, text features, and illustrations.

Lerner Publications Company
A division of Lerner Publishing Group, Inc.
241 First Avenue North
Minneapolis, MN 55401 USA

For reading levels and more information, look up this title at www.lernerbooks.com.

Photos on page 22 are used with the permission of: kanvag/Shutterstock.com (landfill); kipgodi/Shutterstock.com (water); Stockbyte (recycling).

Main body text set in Billy Infant 22/28.
Typeface provided by SparkyType.

Library of Congress Cataloging-in-Publication Data

Library of Congress Cataloging-in-Publication Data
Names: Bullard, Lisa, author. | Thomas, Wes, 1972- illustrator.
Title: Go green by recycling / Lisa Bullard ; illustrated by Wes Thomas.
Description: Minneapolis : Lerner Publications, 2019. | Series: Go green (early bird stories) | Includes bibliographical references and index. | Audience: Ages 5-8. | Audience: Grades K to 3.
Identifiers: LCCN 2018002909 (print) | LCCN 2018002338 (ebook) | ISBN 9781541524866 (eb pdf) | ISBN 9781541520134 (lb : alk. paper) | ISBN 9781541527140 (pb : alk. paper)
Subjects: LCSH: Recycling (Waste, etc.)—Juvenile literature.
Classification: LCC TD794.5 (print) | LCC TD794.5 .B853 2918 (ebook) | DDC 363.72/82—dc23

LC record available at https://lccn.loc.gov/2018002909

Manufactured in the United States of America
1-44349-34595-3/28/2018

TABLE OF CONTENTS

TOO MUCH TRASH

Some kids want to be firefighters. Some kids want to be teachers.

I'm going to be an Earth saver.

People are making an awful lot of trash.
I better take charge!

How do people
make trash?

RECYCLING HELPS CLEAN UP

Mom wants me to clean up my room.

But cleaning my room makes trash.

Recycling will help. *Recycling* means "changing something we don't need into something we can use."

Mom says I can't
recycle my sister.

I can recycle plastic bottles and paper.

And cans and glass too.

Why do people clean up trash?

That way I won't empty
another bottle.

People in a big truck pick up recycling. They take it to a recycling center.

Workers sort recycling into groups.

How can you make less recycling?

CHAPTER 4

SURPRISE!

Companies buy recycling. They might use it to make new cans or paper.

Sometimes they turn recycling into something different. Companies even make T-shirts out of plastic.

This trash problem is
going to take some work.

Maybe you could help by recycling too?

Electronic Recycling

How do people clean up Earth?

LEARN ABOUT RECYCLING

People in the United States are big trash makers. Each person makes more than 4 pounds (1.8 kg) of trash each day.

Some trash is burned. But this makes the air dirty. Some trash is buried. But buried trash can last hundreds of years. And it takes up lots of space.

Some things can be recycled only once. But we can recycle cans many times.

Companies make sandals out of old tires. They make chairs out of old cans. They make carpet out of plastic bottles.

It's good to recycle. It's even better to make less trash. Avoid plastic water bottles. Fill a glass instead.

THINK ABOUT RECYCLING:
CRITICAL-THINKING AND TEXT FEATURE QUESTIONS

What items do you have
that can be recycled?

Do you know ways to have
fun without making trash?

What do the chapter names
tell you about this book?

How can the index help you
read this book?

GLOSSARY

burn: to set something on fire

bury: to dig a hole in the ground, put an object in the hole, and cover it with dirt

plastic: something invented by people that can be made into things such as water bottles and toys

recycle: to turn trash into something that people can use

sort: to separate things into groups

trash: things that people throw away. Trash is also called garbage.

TO LEARN MORE

BOOKS
Devera, Czeena. *Waste and Recycling Collector*. Ann Arbor, MI: Cherry Lake, 2018. Find out how communities collect trash and recycling.

Paul, Miranda. *One Plastic Bag: Isatou Ceesay and the Recycling Women of Gambia*. Minneapolis: Millbrook Press, 2015. Learn how one woman cleaned her town and helped Earth.

WEBSITE
EPA: Recycle City
http://.epa.gov/recyclecity/
This website is from the Environmental Protection Agency. It lets you explore Recycle City through games and activities.

INDEX